The Escape

Dear Dorothy

With ~~fairy~~ best
wishes
love
Hayley
x X x

Lavender Fairy Adventures

The
Escape

Hayley Dartnell

First published by Fuzzy Flamingo 2020
© 2020 Hayley Dartnell

The right of Hayley Dartnell to be identified as author of this
Work has been asserted by her in accordance with sections 77
and 78 of the Copyright, Designs and Patents Act 1988

Paperback ISBN: 978-1-9161147-9-1
Ebook ISBN: 978-1-8380944-0-9

A CIP catalogue record for this book is available from the
British Library

Cover design and typesetting: Fuzzy Flamingo
www.fuzzyflamingo.co.uk

In loving memory of Daphne Dacia Beale
1922 – 1989

Chapter 1

The moth's heart beat loudly as he sat alone on a tree branch in the midst of the shadows. So loud in fact that he thought his antennae would burst with the vibration. Why? Because George the moth had done it, he had finally escaped from the Marsh Beast Gang!

The Marsh Beast Gang are a mixture of rodents, moths and various scary looking creatures. They all live together in the ancient trees and hollowed-out trunks in a shady area of Bluebell Meadow. The gang get up to all sorts of naughty things, as they love to play tricks and silly games. And they have one terrible trait in particular: they steal nectar from the butterflies!

The gang have their own meeting place in which they socialise every evening. It's called the Black Boot Cavern, an abandoned wellington boot, faded to a dark shade of grey. It's full of tiny holes, covered in moss and located next to a very deep swamp.

Earlier that evening, George had watched a popular singing trio set up their equipment in the corner of the Black Boot Cavern. The furry creatures included a bat who couldn't fly, a rat without a tail and a three-legged spider. They would be this evening's entertainment. The moth glanced round the dingy room bustling with creatures eager to see the band perform.

The moth realised that this was a perfect opportunity to run away without being noticed. Taking a deep breath, George casually made his way towards the darkest area of the room. Locating a loose part of the old boot, he lifted the grubby flap just enough to be able to crawl out.

Now hiding under a leaf at the top of the tree, George could hear the muffled sounds of joke-telling and noisy laughter. The Marsh Beasts would party throughout the night. And they'd slurp on the nectar they had stolen from a butterfly earlier that day. George had felt ashamed as he had watched his so-called friends snatch food from the butterfly's grasp and made her cry. Feeling powerless, the moth knew that he couldn't be a part of this horrible gang any longer. There was only one thing to do, and that was to run away.

George gazed up at the late evening sky. Dark blue, dotted with tiny stars and not a cloud in sight. The moth wondered which direction to take. Hoping the full moon would provide an answer, George took a deep breath and fluttered quietly into the night.

Chapter 2

The chatter of hungry starlings looking for their breakfast awoke the moth. Early morning dew had softened the earth, quenching the thirst of the freshly mown lawn in the pretty garden of Crumble Cottage.

George slowly opened his eyes and yawned, unaccustomed to his new surroundings. A dry hollow branch nestled in a cherry tree. The moth had flown as far as he could during the night before finding a safe place to rest.

It was promising to be a bright summer's day, George thought excitedly. He could feel the warmth of the sun already as he took a few tentative steps and peaked over the branch and into the garden. The moth's tummy growled loudly. In his haste to run away, he hadn't eaten the day before, and was now feeling very hungry. So, to his delight, the pretty garden below was full of summer flowers. George left the safety of the tree and flew down to the nearest flowerbed. The moth smiled happily as the floral scent filled his senses as he selected some nectar from the largest flower he could find for his breakfast.

But, before he had the chance to taste the delicious looking pollen, the sunlight surrounding the moth disappeared. The garden grew very dark and George gulped with fear. He turned very slowly to face two pairs of bright green eyes staring straight at him.

6

Chapter 3

Milly the mouse had just finished her breakfast in the garden of Crumble Cottage. The early morning sunshine highlighted her favourite spot to sit. A small fairy cave, covered with moss and overlooking the garden, nestled halfway up the rockery. The cave had formed naturally in amongst the various sized rocks and pebbles that were all stacked on top of each other. Next to it was a small fishpond with a tiny waterfall.

Up until recently, Milly had felt quite safe living in the calm and peaceful garden. But the arrival of two young kittens had made the mouse feel anxious. The human owners were delighted with the lively pair, but Milly knew danger when she saw it. Cats and mice are not a friendly combination. So, the little mouse made sure she kept a safe distance away from them.

As Milly lay in the fairy cave basking in the sunshine, a familiar sound made her ears prick up. It was the sound of the heavy back door opening with a loud creak. This meant only one thing: the kittens were coming out to play!

The inquisitive pair had been introduced to their newly installed cat flap but chose to ignore it. Like most cats, they preferred it when a door was opened for them to be let outside. Milly watched carefully as the mischievous kittens raced across the grass. She heard the back door close firmly behind them and the kitchen window open steadily. The tiny panes of glass each reflected the sunlight.

The warm sweet aroma of freshly baked chocolate cookies filled the garden. The scent made Milly feel hungry again. It was a clear indication that the young woman living in the cottage was making some treats. The mouse decided it was probably much safer for the kittens to be outside anyway. Moments later, Milly's thoughts were confirmed. A loud crash of falling pots and pans came from inside the house.

Blissfully unaware of the kitchen activity,

the kittens carried on playing, until something caught their eye. They jumped excitedly and then pounced on it. The mouse suspected it was just a rose petal that had fallen off one of the bushes. But then she glimpsed a flutter of a silver wing. Milly moved very slowly out of the cave and over the smaller rocks to get a better view. To the mouse's surprise, she could see that the kittens had caught a moth and the poor creature was being treated like a toy.

Taking another step forward, Milly's tiny paw suddenly slipped and nudged a loose pebble from the rockery. The little mouse groaned inwardly with despair as the grey-coloured piece of rock tumbled downwards towards the pond. It landed in the water with a small plop. The noise it made didn't go unnoticed by the kittens. They released the moth immediately and slowly crept towards the pond to investigate. Spotting the mouse poised on a rock, their green eyes grew wide with curiosity. Fearing for her life, Milly scampered off quickly in the direction of the cherry tree. Having fallen onto the wet grass, George seized his chance to escape as well.

Chapter 4

The kittens tentatively sniffed around the rockery, hoping to pick up the scent of the mouse but they couldn't find a trail. They carefully walked around the fishpond, taking extra care not to fall in. Cats by nature are often scared of water and these two were no exception. The furry pair caught sight of their own reflections in the pond and panicked. A terrified meow escaped from each little cat and the frightened duo ran straight back to the cottage. They dived headfirst with speed through the cat flap into the safety of the kitchen. Seconds later, a high-pitched shriek could be heard from the human followed by a further clattering of pans.

From the safety of a branch in the cherry

tree, Milly heard the slamming of the pet door. It swung madly back and forth until it came to a halt. The mouse chuckled at the kittens' crazy antics but she was very concerned about the moth. She had seen the creature fly into the cottage through the open kitchen window. The poor thing was clearly injured as one of his wings wasn't fully outstretched. Milly knew that the moth would find a safe place to hide. But more worryingly the mouse knew that the moth belonged to a gang. The notorious Marsh Beasts that every woodland creature avoids! How had the moth become separated from them, Milly wondered.

There was no time to think about that now. The moth was in pain and he would need help. And kind-hearted Milly knew exactly who to ask.

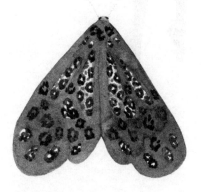

Chapter 5

Nestled deep in the heart of an ancient woodland is a magical place called Bluebell Meadow. It is filled with lakes and streams, an enchanted forest, a bridge and acres of lush green fields. It is home to the Marsh Beasts, all the woodland creatures and most importantly the Lavender Fairies.

A long time ago, a small patch of wild blue flowers suddenly appeared during the month of May. The petals bloomed brightly amongst the stone ruins of where a monastery once stood. But this expanse of land didn't have a proper name. So, in honour of the pretty bell-shaped flowers, the local human residents decided to call it Bluebell Meadow.

But why did the bluebells only grow in that

particular area? According to folklore, it is the final resting place of a wise woman; also known as the local Witch. Hundreds of years ago, the witch used to live in the woods with her black cat. She had a kind and gentle soul and spent her days mixing up special potions. These were to treat the local residents when they had an illness, a bit like a doctor who gives you medicine when you are not feeling very well.

But legend could also make you believe that the witch had transformed herself into a bluebell when she died. But what happened to her black cat? Nobody knows. Every year thereafter during the month of May, lots of bluebells happily grow in that spot. Perhaps there is magic in the soil as the flowers always look like they are smiling. But to this day the mystery still remains.

Milly bounded across the meadow with speed, ignoring the beautiful yellow dandelions and white daisies that carpeted the ground. Acorn Café was in sight and she needed to get there fast!

Chapter 6

Everyone's favourite place to eat in Bluebell Meadow is Acorn Café. A secret meeting place that lays hidden from the eyes of humans. Tucked within the roots of a beautiful oak tree, standing proud in the centre of the meadow. Some believe that the tree roots are buried so deep that it continues to grow and is over a thousand years old.

The café is run by Mrs Woolley. A wise old fairy-mouse and her young apprentice Tuppence the Lavender Fairy. Together they bake cakes and savoury snacks from the food that the woodland creatures bring them each day. Everyone is welcome to share the food apart from the Marsh Beast Gang.

The lake that surrounds the café is

affectionately known as Weeping Willow Pond. It was given its name due to the gnarly weeping willow tree that is situated on the opposite side of the bank. Ducks, swans and moorhens live nearby in the tall grass by the water's edge.

As the sun grew higher, the temperature grew hotter. But Milly carried on running as fast as her little legs would go. She needed the help of her friend, a small brown bird called Jenny Wren. And Acorn Café was the place to find her!

Chapter 7

Acorn Café was full of hungry customers when Milly arrived. Feeling very hot and bothered, she quickly scanned the open-air picnic area and spotted Mrs Woolley. The fairy-mouse was busy clearing tables and mopping up spills. Milly's best friend Tuppence was behind the serving counter. The fairy was expertly pouring fresh nettle tea into an empty acorn that was fashioned into a small cup.

Tuppence felt Milly's presence and glanced towards the entrance of the café. Their eyes locked onto one another immediately and broke into smiles. The young fairy instinctively knew who the mouse was looking for.

"You will find Jenny Wren with the blackbird sisters," yelled Tuppence, over the din of the noisy eaters. She nodded her head in the direction of Weeping Willow Pond.

"Thank you!" squeaked Milly, waving her little paw. The mouse spotted the tiny bird perched on a log near the water's edge, chatting happily to the sisters, Bibi and Bow. Milly grinned as she hastily weaved her way towards them.

Chapter 8

The trio were delighted to see Milly. They all flapped their wings with excitement, almost sending the slice of Mrs Woolley's seed cake they were sharing flying off into the pond. But clever Bibi caught the savoury snack in her beak just in the nick of time. The greedy ducks quacked loudly with disappointment when the freebie didn't come their way.

"I knew I would find you here, Jenny!" Milly exclaimed breathlessly, nodding hello to the blackbird sisters. The mouse took a seat beside the little bird and sat quietly until she regained her breath. Bibi, the eldest of the blackbird sisters, encouraged the mouse to take a sip of water from her saucer. Milly accepted it gratefully.

Sensing that something was wrong, three pairs of eyes stared intently at Milly, waiting for her to speak.

"A moth was injured this morning at Crumble Cottage," whispered Milly. The birds all stared at the mouse in shock. Instinct told them the creature was from the Marsh Beast Gang. "I suspect he has a broken wing and will need help." Milly glanced nervously around her. "Please can you get a message to the Lavender Fairies?" she asked the tiny brown bird hopefully.

When a woodland creature is in danger or requires help, Jenny Wren will take a message to the fairies who live in Toadstool Hall; a bit like a postman who delivers your parcels. Jenny agreed immediately and kindly pushed the plate towards Milly, offering to share the tasty snack.

"Tell us everything that has happened since breakfast time, Milly," Bow the younger blackbird sister suggested, her voice full of concern.

Anxious for the information not to be overheard by the customers of Acorn Café, the friends gathered closer. Milly helped herself to a crumb of the delicious cake and started from the beginning.

Chapter 9

George the Moth lay wide awake. From the safety of the spare room in which he was hiding, George could hear the humans sleeping soundly. Their gentle snores floated down the hallway whilst the kittens purred softly. They lay curled up together in their basket on the landing.

It had taken George a considerable amount of time to make his way to the upper floor of the cottage. But he had found a wardrobe to shelter in. The wooden double doors had been open just wide enough for George to flutter inside and onto a shelf. It was filled with neatly folded blankets and winter clothing. In the lower section of the cupboard a selection of coats and jackets hung from a rail. Exhausted, George had nestled himself as comfortably as he could onto a very soft fluffy jumper.

In normal circumstances, the moth would have been joyful at the prospect of nibbling on the feast of yarn that lay before him. But not today. George simply wasn't interested. All he could feel was the pain of his broken wing inflicted by those two naughty kittens.

Did you know that moths are famous for nibbling clothes that are stored in a wardrobe or a cupboard? Well, the next time you reach for your favourite jumper, take a close look at it. If you find any tiny holes in the fabric then you'll know a moth has taken a bite.

The grandfather clock in the downstairs hallway gently chimed eleven o'clock. George counted each beat slowly. The Marsh Beast Gang would be gathered in the Black Boot Cavern for the nightly entertainment. And someone would surely note George's absence. But they wouldn't know that the moth had run away and was injured. George's newly found freedom was suddenly not so appealing. Realising he needed help and having no one else to turn to, he let out a distress call, hoping that someone would come to his rescue.

Chapter 10

As promised, Jenny Wren had set off for Toadstool Hall, home to the Lavender Fairies.

It's a beautiful tree house, deep in the heart of the enchanted forest of Bluebell Meadow. Their magical home is hidden inside the trunk of a hawthorn tree and surrounded by a carpet of fungi. A variety of wild mushrooms that grow in damp and mossy areas of the forest. The exact location of Toadstool Hall is a secret one and known to very few of the woodland creatures. The hawthorn tree is protected by a magic spell created by the Lavender Fairies. An invisible bubble surrounds the tree to keep them all safe from harm and unwanted visitors.

Only chosen friends of the fairies are allowed

inside Toadstool Hall, accessed by a secret doorway. It leads into a wide hallway where you are greeted by a talking mirror. On the ground floor you'll find a large kitchen where all the fairies gather to eat around the big, round wooden table. Next door to the kitchen is an apothecary room. The elder fairies use this room to create their magical potions and recipes. Throughout the treehouse, you'll find spiral staircases connecting the floors together. With lots of bedrooms, nooks and window seats all cleverly carved from the wood of the tree. Over time, the fairies have collected and lovingly repurposed twigs, moss, feathers and wool and made it into furniture.

On the lower ground level, they have their own secret walled garden. It's dotted with small areas in which to write, sew, study and paint. A generous fruit and vegetable patch lies in the sunniest area. It provides the fairies with food to eat all year round.

Lyra, Queen of the Lavender Fairies, was in her study. She sat at her desk and glanced out of the window. The sun had set early that day behind some angry looking clouds. A storm was brewing and Lyra was beginning to worry. She knew that the little bird was on her way with an important message and was concerned for her safety. The Forest like any other could be a dangerous place to be on your own, especially at night. Feeling a sudden chill, the fairy got up from her chair. The pale cream lace skirt of her dress fell just below her knees. Lyra pulled a small patchwork blanket off the sofa and wrapped it around her shoulders. It bunched her long white curly pigtails inside the fabric, but Lyra didn't mind one bit.

Lyra is a powerful fairy and full of great knowledge and, together with Mrs Woolley, they run Toadstool Hall. A Lavender Fairy's life is very busy. But they are the most helpful ladies you could ever wish to meet. Each fairy has their own unique magical powers and can cure many illnesses. They always have time to listen, to share a cup of tea and simply be a good friend. Their kindness and positivity is well known throughout Bluebell Meadow. Unlike their arch enemies the Marsh Beast Gang, who do their utmost to cause pain and misery to others.

A Lavender Fairy wears a handmade dress created from repurposed fabric, unique to their own style and personality. On their heads they wear bobble hats made from recycled yarn that they have found. Each one works as a torchlight, which is very useful at night. Instead of wands, the fairies carry a small handbag. Inside each bag you will find all sorts of things, including a gazing ball. The ball itself works a bit like a telephone. You gently tap twice on the glass and say out loud the person's name who you wish to speak to. Then wait a moment or two and that person will appear inside the glass.

So why are they called Lavender Fairies?

It's simple, really. Every fairy was born with a sprig of lavender in her tummy. Whilst lavender itself has many healing properties, the fragrance of the flower can help you sleep. It is often worn as a perfume or made into soap. But overall, lavender is a well-known natural deterrent to keep moths away from nibbling clothes. Knitted woollen clothes in particular.

Moths do not like the smell of lavender, as it makes them very poorly. So, if you are worried about your clothes in the wardrobe, ask a grown up to help. Simply pop a handful of dried lavender flowers into a bag made from fabric and hang it inside. It will keep those naughty moths away for good.

Lyra got up and paced the floor. Mrs Woolley appeared in the doorway with a teapot in her hand, her face full of concern for the little bird's safety. The fairy-mouse refilled their empty acorn cups with soothing chamomile tea. She took a seat by the fireplace and blew gently on the hot liquid in her teacup.

"The little bird will arrive soon," said Mrs Woolley all matter of fact, taking a seat on the small overstuffed sofa. Lyra nodded in agreement and went to join her. All they could do was wait.

Chapter 11

A short while later, the little bird came tumbling through the open window and into Lyra's study. Startled at Jenny's unusual method of entry, both fairies jumped up quickly from the sofa. Lyra just managed to catch a vase of flowers that was about to fall off her desk that Jenny had knocked into.

"Sorry I'm so late!" Jenny squeaked. The little bird was completely out of breath.

Lyra embraced her feathered friend, grateful of her safe arrival, then put the vase back in its rightful place.

"Are you okay, Jenny?" Lyra asked.

"We were very worried about you flying through the forest at this time of night," Mrs Woolley added. "I'll go and get you a drink of water."

Jenny nodded her acceptance of the offer of refreshment.

"My usual way in through the secret doorway was blocked, Lyra. Someone has trampled on some of the mushrooms," the little bird said worriedly as Mrs Woolley returned to the study and proffered a saucer of water to quench Jenny's thirst. Thanking the fairy-mouse, the grateful little bird took a long drink of water and hiccupped loudly. The fairies shared a knowing look as Jenny's eyes twinkled with embarrassment.

"We'll take care of the doorway, Jenny, but in the meantime, who needs our help?" Lyra asked, as she placed a plump handmade cushion next to the small fireplace for Jenny to sit on. The little bird always favoured it as it was stuffed with wool that had been gathered from the stiles in the neighbouring fields.

The Lavender Fairies sat down once again on the comfy sofa covered with colourful crocheted blankets. They listened carefully as Jenny repeated, word for word, the information from Milly the Mouse.

Chapter 12

As the sun began to rise in Bluebell Meadow, Toadstool Hall was alive with activity. Last night, Lyra had devised a plan in which to help rescue the moth. The assignment had been given to fellow friend, Apple the Lavender Fairy. So, the woodland treehouse was now preparing for Apple's departure.

All the fairies had enjoyed an early breakfast together of fresh strawberries and peppermint tea in the sunny kitchen. Everyone knew the plan and they waited for Apple to finish getting ready.

Apple, as you've probably guessed, is named after a popular piece of fruit. And she always wears a pale green dress that is embellished with a small pink button at the neckline.

As she stood in front of the talking mirror in the hallway, Apple smoothed down her dress and adjusted her bobble hat. A small pink creation, hand-crocheted, just like Lyra's, but in a different colour with a matching flower on it.

The fairy smiled with satisfaction as the mirror nodded its approval with a wink.

Apple's crocheted bag, also in pink, was sitting on the half-moon-shaped table looking very heavy. It had been packed by Mrs Woolley and was bulging at the seams. The housekeeper had filled it with food and essentials that the magical fairy would need for this job. Apple eyed it warily, wondering if she was going to be able to fly with such a large bag to carry.

"Are you ready to go, Apple?" Lyra asked as she stepped out from her study and into the entrance hall. The magical hallway gently expanded to accommodate Mrs Woolley and all the fairies that had gathered to bid farewell.

"Yes, I am," Apple said cheerfully. Suddenly realising the weight of her overstuffed bag, she whispered the words, "Weight be gone." In an instant, the woollen bag resized itself back to its normal shape and felt as light as a feather.

Lyra hugged her friend goodbye then

watched as Apple stood on the doorstep of Toadstool Hall and shook out her long, white curly pigtails. They transformed immediately into huge translucent wings. The fairy took off in the direction of Crumble Cottage to a chorus of goodbyes from the Lavender Fairy Clan that sent her smiling all the way.

Chapter 13

Inside the confines of the wardrobe, George was becoming very thirsty. Surely someone had heard his cry for help and would soon come to his rescue?

Wincing with pain, George tried to spread his very limp broken wing, but it was useless. The kittens had been chasing each other up and down the stairs all morning. George couldn't run the risk of venturing out. The fear of being captured again was simply overwhelming. Feeling scared and all alone, the moth snuggled deeper into the safety of the jumper. Silent tears welled up in his eyes as he laid his head on the softness of the yarn. But then suddenly George heard a flutter of wings that he did not recognise. He blinked away his tears when he heard a gentle voice call out to him.

"Hello?" said a friendly voice as the cupboard doors slowly opened, letting in a shaft of light. "I've come to help."

Relief washed over the moth, grateful that his prayers had been answered. But that comfort soon vanished when he found himself face to face with an arch enemy. A Lavender Fairy!

Chapter 14

A very long time ago, a gang of moths called Nock-two-dee had broken into Emerald Castle, in the land of St Avalawn. A gang leader named Dark Arches had led his friends deep inside the ancient palace one stormy night for shelter. Whilst searching for food, the hungry gang of moths had found the bedroom of the high priestess who lived there. The gang had found several of her beautiful silk dresses laying inside an open wooden chest. Then set about nibbling on them greedily.

When the high priestess discovered her clothes in ruins, she knew they were beyond repair. The luxurious material was covered in tiny holes. Knowing that only a moth would do this type of damage, she knew exactly who could help find the culprits. The Lavender Fairies. The high priestess immediately called upon the services of little Jenny Wren to deliver the message asking for help.

Sunflower the Lavender Fairy had insisted on accompanying Lyra to Emerald Castle. After many days of searching, they had discovered the gang hidden in a disused linen cupboard in the depths of the castle. When confronted with their crime, the moths had shown no remorse. But the scent from the Lavender Fairies severely weakened their strength and the moths were unable to fly.

As punishment, the angry priestess banished the moths from the land of St Avalawn. She sent them to a cave, deep within a haunted forest. She placed a curse on them all should they ever escape.

But from that moment on, Dark Arches vowed he would get his revenge on the Lavender Fairies one day. The legendary story of the Nock-two-dee gang is well known throughout Bluebell Meadow. And to this day, the animosity between the moths and the Lavender Fairies still continues. But for how long?

Chapter 15

George felt the colour drain from his face as the little fairy fluttered onto the neatly folded jumper. Smiling happily at the moth, her wings transformed back into their curly pigtails. She secured each one with a pink hair bobble before straightening her hat.

"Hi, I'm Apple." The fairy introduced herself with a smile and held out her tiny hand. "And you must be George?" She held her smile in place.

The injured moth ignored her hand as the story of Dark Arches coursed through his veins. Common sense told George that the fairy was here to help him, but still he was frightened. The moth nodded, unable to speak. But what was the alternative? He couldn't fly! It was either face potential capture and torture from the kittens or accept help he desperately needed from the fairy.

Apple read the moth's anxious thoughts and took a few steps backwards to give him some space. Knowing he was hungry, she began unpacking her pink crocheted bag. George's tummy rumbled as Apple revealed the feast of flower heads that Mrs Woolley had kindly provided. He looked longingly at the sight of the nectar that peeped through the petals.

"Here you go, George," Apple said, kindly offering him a bright yellow flower and nodding encouragingly. George accepted it, then remembered his manners. He croaked a thank you before devouring the pollen.

"When you're ready, I'll take a look at that wing," Apple said with an extra grin. "I've got a potion in my bag that will heal that up just nicely!"

Chapter 16

"Argh!" roared Blackskull, a large angry moth, his eyes blazing wildly. The vibration of his voice caused the grubby vessel he was holding full of nectar to slosh over the sides. It spilled over onto the battered corkscrew being used as a table. The head of the Marsh Beast Gang couldn't believe what he had just heard from one of his spies. The Rat scuttled away into the shadows of the Black Boot Cavern after delivering the news of George's disappearance.

Silence fell amongst the woodland creatures within. The news had spread across Bluebell Meadow that George was missing. And a rumour was circulating that a Lavender Fairy was with the moth. *But why?* thought Blackskull.

The Escape

Since that fateful day when his great uncle had crossed paths with the Lavender Fairies at Emerald Castle, life had changed. And the Marsh Beasts had kept their distance from the magical beings that lived in in the enchanted forest.

Blackskull was thinking quickly; he needed a plan to rescue George before the fairies weakened his immune system. And Blackskull would not let history repeat itself again. The silence in the cavern was slowly lifting and was replaced with hushed whispers instead. The legend of Blackskull's famous ancestor was now the talk of the tavern. Voices grew louder and questions began to fly around the dingy drinking establishment. Would Dark Arches and his crew return to Bluebell Meadow, perhaps? Did they have enough strength to fly from the cave they had been banished to? How would they escape? And would they bestow their ultimate revenge on the Lavender Fairies?

Blackskull listened gravely to the chatter and, for the first time in his life, he felt afraid. Very afraid.

Chapter 17

Over at Crumble Cottage, George's wing was healing nicely. The moth could now manage a short and gentle flutter under the Lavender Fairy's watchful eye. Whatever 'magic potion' that Apple kept dabbing on it from a tiny glass bottle was clearly working. As were the flowers that were full of nectar. Having been selected by Mrs Woolley they contained special healing powers to restore the moth's wing quickly back to health.

After a slightly awkward start, the moth and the fairy had formed a mutual friendship. Through a genuine love of books and reading. History books in particular. Apple had pulled out a homemade quilt from her bag for them both to rest on inside the cupboard. Adding lots of cushions for George's comfort. They were now surrounded by literature that had weighed down Apple's bag making it so heavy. The fairy-mouse had thought of everything for this special assignment. George, however, was simply amazed. He watched avidly every time Apple opened her magical case, wondering what she would pull out next.

After a day or two, the conversation between moth and fairy flowed easily. Their chatter soon turned towards the Marsh Beast Gang. George's eyes clouded over when he spoke and he freely admitted his secret to Apple of running away from them. The moth had fallen into some very bad habits being part of the gang, which he knew had been wrong. But the right thing to do was to leave. He had explained the painful scenario about what had happened with the peacock butterfly and the nectar. George was feeling stronger each day and was determined to start a new life elsewhere before it was too late.

"But how, Apple?" George asked quietly, unable to make eye contact and still feeling ashamed of his past wrongdoings.

Having listened intently to George's confession, the little fairy formed a plan. They would just need a bit of help and a gazing ball.

Chapter 18

Toadstool Hall was alive with anticipation. Apple had spoken with Lyra through her gazing ball to finalise their escape plan for George. As you know, to us humans it looks like a tiny glass marble and every Lavender Fairy has one. They use it as their communication tool. It works a bit like a mobile phone, so the fairies can see and hear each other through the glass. They gently tap the ball twice and say the person's name out loud who they wish to speak to. Easy!

By the phase of the next new moon, Apple and George would be leaving Crumble Cottage. The residents of Bluebell Meadow were now on high alert as rumours spread of a return by the infamous Dark Arches and the Nock-two-dee gang was likely. The Lavender Fairies wanted to be prepared for every eventuality. So they advised all the woodland creatures to be careful over the next few days.

Whilst Apple prepared lunch the day before their departure, the fairy sensed that George was feeling anxious.

"I shall miss you, Apple. You have become a very good friend to me," the moth said quietly, a tear forming in his eye.

"Oh, George, and I shall miss you too. But you have learnt the error of your ways, so be proud of that. Just have faith that everything will work out okay," Apple said reassuringly, offering George a flower.

"Now eat," the fairy declared with a huge grin. "You need to keep your strength up!"

After lunch, whilst George enjoyed a nap, Apple went through the plan again in her head. But something bright caught her eye. It was George's wings, they were gently glowing as he slept. Apple smiled happily as she watched them heal before her very eyes. The power of the lavender was clearly working and dancing merrily through the moth's veins like tiny silver threads.

Tomorrow would soon arrive and they would be ready.

Chapter 19

Large black rain clouds gathered and a fierce wind howled with frustration throughout the haunted forest. The cries of the resident jackdaws could be heard as they circled high above the tree tops. The full moon that had shone brightly just days before had vanished. A storm was imminent and all the wild animals were taking shelter.

Dark Arches stood in the doorway of the cave and looked out across the sky, waiting to see a glimpse of the new moon. His excitement was growing. He couldn't wait to escape this dreadful place in which they had all been confined for so long. "This time tomorrow we will be in Bluebell Meadow," the moth muttered quietly to himself. But the time could not come quick enough. The ugly moth glanced over at his friends who were busy planning on how to celebrate their much-awaited freedom.

Confinement in the cave had taken its tolls on the moths. It had turned them into menacing-looking creatures. Their soft brown wings were much darker in colour and had grown larger and coarser. The delicate antennae were now contorted and wiry. Bulging from their sockets were beady eyes, twisting their features into terrifying masks. The moths didn't feel any remorse for their part in destroying those beautiful dresses owned by the high priestess. Why should they? It had been fun and they had been hungry! If it hadn't been for those meddling fairies, they would not have been found at all. Their lavender scent had severely weakened their strength and immune systems, leaving them all unable to fly for many years.

Up until now.

A spy of Dark Arches who lived in the woods had arrived a few days earlier with two pieces of news. The first bit was about the death of the high priestess. A mysterious fire had broken out at Emerald Castle. Her highness had been trapped in the tower and unable to escape the flames. This meant that the curse bestowed on the moths had been lifted! But Dark Arches' happiness was short lived. Upon hearing about the disappearance of a moth from the Marsh Beast Gang, his joy turned to fury. He was immediately suspicious and suspected that the Lavender Fairies were involved. This had spurred the moth's act of revenge to a higher level. So with their strength now fully restored, it was time to pay a visit to Bluebell Meadow.

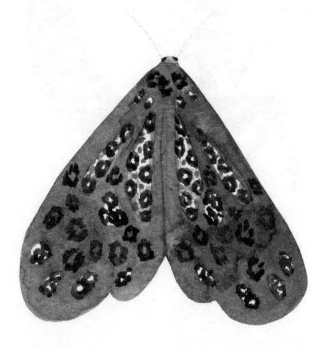

Chapter 20

The new moon had appeared briefly in a rare break of the storm clouds that had amassed. Blackskull watched as she disappeared behind them again as the wind gathered speed. Well aware that they were running out of time, the moth was becoming incredibly anxious. As each moment passed, Blackskull instinctively knew that Dark Arches and his gang were on their way. The sudden death of the high priestess meant that the Nock-two-dee gang were free and were heading to Bluebell Meadow.

The Marsh Beasts had finally located George's whereabouts and were camped out on a branch of the cherry tree. Unable to gain entry into Crumble Cottage, they huddled close together to shield themselves from the wind. The weather had suddenly taken a turn for the worse and the lady owner had closed the kitchen window with a bang. All other possible routes were blocked including the chimney. The only way in was a dangerous one – through the cat flap!

Blackskull fluttered down from the branch to the ledge of the kitchen window. Peering through the small pane of glass, he observed the two sleeping kittens curled up in a cardboard box together. It was by the old-fashioned-looking cooker known as an AGA. They didn't stir when the grandfather clock downstairs chimed, indicating it was eleven o'clock. But it certainly made the moth jump with fright.

Regaining his composure, Blackskull sighed with despair. How were they going to get in and save George? They needed help. Help from the Lavender Fairies. Meaning they would have to work side by side. Was that even possible? Blackskull frantically racked his brains for another solution. But there wasn't one. They were all in danger because with the Nock-two-dee gang's strength fully restored, they were capable of anything. Blackskull knew that Dark Arches and his friends would claim the Black

Boot Cavern for themselves, forcing out the Marsh Beast Gang. The vengeful moths would cruelly issue punishment should anyone stand up to them. Their aim would be to rule Bluebell Meadow, not stopping until they made every woodland creature's life a misery. With the Lavender Fairies suffering the most under their reign of terror.

Chapter 21

The Nock-two-dee gang had taken to the skies. Persistent heavy raindrops fell onto their hardy wings, bouncing off like tiny crystals into the trees below. As the wind picked up speed, it whipped savagely at their bodies as they soared through the forest. They cleverly dodged the outstretched branches that were desperately trying to catch them.

The moths all heard the distant rumble of thunder and forged their way ahead through the biting storm. Twisting and turning as they flew, they eventually left the forest behind them. They travelled across several counties with the taste of revenge in their mouths until Bluebell Meadow was in sight.

Chapter 22

The Blackbird sisters shook the raindrops off their wings before taking their positions on the highest branch of the cherry tree. They chirruped loudly and clearly over the noise of the rain. Their combined warning call signalled to everyone that the Nock-two-dee gang were near.

Down below on the windowsill, Blackskull closed his eyes with despair as he heard the birds' chorus. He sat motionless under a battered basil plant, the damp leaves providing a little shelter.

For the first time, the moth was not concerned for his own safety but of those around him. Blackskull was willing to sacrifice his own life to save his friend George and the lives of the Lavender Fairies.

Deep down the moth knew that the residents of Bluebell Meadow relied on the Lavender Fairies. And right now, he needed them too. By asking for their help it would mean his own strength would be weakened immediately if he came into contact with them. It was a risk Blackskull wanted to take.

As the moth listened again to a more urgent call from the blackbirds, Blackskull also heard a different noise. The gentle sound of wings fluttering. Flying towards him was Lyra, Queen of the Lavender Fairies. His silent plea just moments before had been answered as he caught the distinct aroma of lavender. Now scared for his life, he squeezed his eyes tightly shut, waiting for the compounds of the fragrance to hit his senses. Within minutes, the moth's body would be immobilised. Blackskull waited, but nothing was happening, and after a few seconds he opened his eyes. He felt okay. What was going on? He looked at Lyra for an answer as she stood before him.

"Hello Blackskull," Lyra said, reading his thoughts. "Do not be afraid of the lavender, it will not harm you as I am here to help."

Lyra stepped onto the ledge, the tiny raindrops on her gossamer wings sparkled with light. The moth gazed at the fairy in awe and immediately offered his antenna to shake the fairy's outstretched hand.

"Thank you, Lyra," said the moth gratefully. Never had he been so pleased to see a fairy.

Chapter 23

Earlier that day, Apple had watched the residents of Crumble Cottage climb into a taxi and drive away. From the spare room window, the fairy had seen the couple load just one small suitcase into the boot of the car. It had just started raining and a neighbour appeared alongside the vehicle carrying a large umbrella. A small white dog was at his heels. The conversation between the humans only lasted a few minutes and was muffled due to the howling wind. The little dog had glanced up at the window, barked at Apple, then winked. He was trying to tell her something. But before they could communicate, the neighbour had scooped up his pet and marched briskly off down the street.

The clue was in the luggage, Apple realised. So the humans would only be away for a short time. Therefore leaving the kittens in the capable hands of the neighbour who would pop in to feed them. That is what the little dog was trying to relay. But why?

Apple was still pondering on the encounter when downstairs clock in the hallway struck midnight. The sound of the first chime echoed faintly up the stairwell. "George, it's time to go," Apple whispered.

The moth nodded in agreement as the fairy picked up her crocheted bag with her right hand. Then she tapped the flower on her bobble hat with her left. It lit up immediately and acted as a torchlight. As planned, George hopped onto Apple's back, and clung to her wings.

Exiting the cupboard and into the spare room, they paused on the threshold to check the hallway. The kittens were nowhere in sight. Apple and George would have to be extra careful as they flew down the stairs and headed towards the kitchen.

Apple knew from her previous conversation with Lyra that there was only one way out of the cottage. And it was through the cat flap.

The small pet doorway was being held

open with twigs that the Blackbird sisters had gathered. They had managed to construct a prop to wedge it open whilst the kittens were asleep elsewhere. But how long would the twigs hold out?

Chapter 24

"Well, well, well!" boomed a loud, angry voice.

Blackskull slowly turned to face his ancestor. The windowsill was slippery from heavy rain as it trickled down each individual pane of the glass.

"In cahoots with the Lavender Fairies now, are we?" snarled Dark Aches, his eyes blazing in disgust. "I'm ashamed to call you my relative. No moth can be friends with a Lavender Fairy!" Dark Arches cried, his face raging with anger. It looked far more terrifying in the pouring rain. A bolt of lightning tore through the sky, illuminating the garden and magnifying the shadow of the gruesome moth. Blackskull took a tentative step backwards, trying to ignore the elder moth's harsh words.

"What sort of Marsh Beast does that make you?" the older moth's voice screamed. His voice rose a few more decibels. Blackskull was unable to speak, terrified of his great uncle and his gang. They surrounded Blackskull, crushing the smaller moth up against the windowpane, knocking a small flowerpot to the ground. The terracotta vessel smashed into pieces as it landed with a thud on a concrete slab. From the branch of the cherry tree, the Marsh Beasts saw their leader was in trouble. They huddled together and flew down to rescue him.

Chapter 25

In the house next door to Crumble Cottage, the small white dog growled quietly in his basket. He didn't like thunderstorms. But as heavy rain thrashed against the windows there was something else that was bothering him.

"What is it, old boy?" murmured his pet owner Fred. The old man stirred comfortably in his armchair by the fireplace, having fallen asleep whilst listening to an article on the radio. The sound of a flowerpot shattering outside made the small dog sit up straight and lift his ears. He began woofing loudly, just as a bolt of lightning streaked through the open curtains of the living room.

Feeling uneasy, Fred got to his feet. He

walked over to the window and drew the curtains together. "Come on, Topper, let's pop next door and check that everything's okay."

The little dog didn't hesitate and ran out into the hallway. Sensing trouble, he eagerly awaited his master to open the front door.

Fred had promised Chloe his neighbour that he would feed the kittens whilst they were away for the night. So a final check next door would put his mind at rest. Pulling on a large waterproof jacket, he reached inside the deep pocket for the spare key to Crumble Cottage. Smiling, Fred went to open the front door. But the noise of Topper's claws scratching at the utility cupboard door stopped him.

"Good thinking, old boy!" said the old man, spearing his dark green fishing umbrella from inside the cupboard. It was now dry from the downpour earlier that afternoon. Pulling up his hood, Fred opened the front door and the little dog bounded down the path. So fast, in fact, that he didn't hear Fred shout, "Wait for me!"

Chapter 26

Lyra spotted the winged duo enter the kitchen. She watched as they settled behind the cluster of cereal boxes on top of the fridge. The Queen of the Lavender Fairies was on the opposite side of the room. Hiding between a pink teapot and a stack of patterned china teacups. All vintage style Lyra had noted appreciatively. Then she quickly turned her attention to the drama that was unfolding in the garden. The moths were still arguing, meaning Apple and George could safely make their getaway out of the cat flap. Lyra was just about to give the go-ahead signal to Apple when a huge clap of thunder ripped through Bluebell Meadow. It awoke the sleeping kittens from their basket by the cooker. Then they heard a small gasp of shock. Their sharp eyes quickly scanned the kitchen and pinpointed Lyra's whereabouts! The small cats could see the fairy's attention was diverted and stealthily inched their way over the floor, then jumped silently onto the worktop behind the white magical being.

Lyra didn't sense the two black furry creatures until a small black paw was reaching towards her. The sharp claws were extended and waving excitedly. Lyra ducked behind the teapot just in time to see the paw knock over the stack of pretty teacups. All six of them skittered at first, then rolled lazily back and forth in a half circular motion. Making their way to the edge of the worktop, gravity finally pulled each one crashing to the quarry-tiled floor.

Chapter 27

Hearing the crash of china, Apple peeped out carefully from behind the cluster of cereal boxes. She accidentally knocked the flower on her bobble hat in the process. She watched as Lyra flew up to the top of a cupboard. Away from the kitten's outstretched paws that were trying to catch her.

Apple tried to weigh up their chance to escape. She glanced out of the window and into the garden. To the little green fairy's horror, a silver mass of wings was forming a ball and it was heading straight towards the kitchen window. It was following the beam of light projecting from Apple's hat! Realising her mistake, Apple tapped the flower to extinguish the light, but it was too late! All the Moths had naturally migrated towards it at speed and hurled themselves straight through the pane of glass.

Chapter 28

"Who's there?!" the next-door neighbour yelled, hearing the glass smash as he closed the front door with a slam. Fearing it could be a burglar, Fred kept hold of his wet umbrella. Droplets of water formed a trail as he marched briskly down the narrow hallway. There was no reply to his question. The cottage was silent. Fred stood in the kitchen and switched on the lights. Scratching his head in bewilderment, the old man saw the fragments of china and glass all over the floor. At the sight of the tall dark-hooded figure standing in the doorway, chaos erupted!

Spying the two kittens crouching in a corner trembling with fright, the little dog began barking at them. Hissing back in defiance, they zig-zagged their way across the kitchen to make a bid for freedom. The dog followed the pair in hot pursuit, almost knocking poor Fred over. The three small furry creatures dived through the open cat flap with such force that the twigs snapped instantly. The magnetic door, having been set free, swung madly back and forth, finally locking itself shut after several seconds.

As Fred regained his balance, the huge ball of moths quickly disbanded across the low-level ceiling. As the energy bulbs became brighter, the tiny winged creatures aimed for every possible bit of light they could reach.

Apple could not see another way out. They would surely be spotted if she risked flying across the kitchen. "What shall we do?" she asked Lyra telepathically, hidden from sight and back behind the cereal boxes waiting for Lyra to respond.

"Just stay calm, both of you, all will be okay!" said the Queen of the Lavender Fairies.

And strangely enough, George heard the message too.

Chapter 29

Surprised by this sudden attack of moths, Fred automatically began batting them away with his hands. They flew around the kitchen in such a frenzy that they bounced off the neighbour's head. Reaching for his wet umbrella, the neighbour opened it halfway. Aiming it at the ceiling, Fred flapped the wet weather instrument in their direction, coaxing them all towards the back door. Turning the key in the lock, the old man then reached for the door handle. Pulling it open, he shooed out the silver creatures into the raging storm.

Seizing their opportunity to leave, Apple spread her wings once more. George was holding tightly as they took flight from the fridge. But in their haste to get away, Apple's magic handbag knocked over all the cereal boxes. Like a row of dominos, each packet of oats, puffed rice and flakes of corn began to topple over, the contents flying up into the air. Fred watched in bewilderment as the dried breakfast food gently peppered the kitchen floor, just like confetti.

"Oh my goodness!" the old man cried at this further commotion, carefully tiptoeing around the carpet of cereal to search for a broom.

But what happened next surprised Fred the most. It was the sight of the little green fairy flying towards him carrying a moth on her back. A moment later, another fairy appeared. She simply floated down in what could only be described as a white vision from the top of a cupboard!

Absolutely flabbergasted, Fred stood rooted to the spot. His mouth hung open in utter astonishment and allowed his eyes to follow the tiny trio as far as the kitchen door. They turned and hovered briefly on the threshold.

"Thank you, Fred!" the magical beings sang. They waved in gratitude before disappearing into the night.

Chapter 30

The Blackbird sisters sat waiting patiently under a hedge near the fishpond. Their job was to escort George to his new home. But they didn't have much time. So, after exchanging fond farewells, George thanked them all once again for their kindness and generosity.

"I won't forget what you all did for me," George said kindly, patting Apple's hand with his antenna.

"You're most welcome, George," Apple replied, tucking George safely under the wing of the youngest Blackbird sister. Bow stretched out her wings ready to fly.

"Go!" encouraged Lyra in a low voice. "And stay safe, all of you."

With a flap of their wings, the birds set off. The rain had eased but danger was still lurking. A rustle from behind indicated they were not alone. Milly slipped quietly away into the shadows as Lyra and Apple turned to face Blackskull.

"Did George escape?" the head of the Marsh Beast gang asked quietly, keeping his voice to a murmur.

Both fairies nodded as Blackskull thanked them.

"But you must leave immediately," the moth added. "You remember the curse? Dark Arches is still out there. Go, before he sees you both," he whispered urgently as a cry from the darkness rang out.

"This isn't the end!" Dark Arches cried out from the shadows. "We will be back to have our revenge on all of you, then you'll be sorry!"

The moth's final words echoed into the night sky.

Epilogue

After a long trip through the night, George and the Blackbird sisters arrived at their destination; a disused lighthouse situated on the Norfolk Coast. An area rich with history and surrounded by far reaching fields. A perfect retreat for a quiet old moth to spend his twilight years.

As the sun began to rise in the beautiful seaside village of Old Honeystone, George took a deep breath and savoured the salty sea air.

But what will this new life mean for George the moth? Will magic and mystery come knocking when he makes a new friend… Stay tuned.

About the Author

After leaving behind the corporate world of working in London, Hayley Dartnell found herself in lockdown writing a short story about a little cloth doll she made. A true believer in fairytales and all things magical, her imagination went into overdrive as she listened to her inner child speak. She divides her time between Devon and Cambridgeshire.

To see the Lavender Fairies brought to life visit their Instagram page:

www.instagram.com/lavenderfairyadventures